KYLIE

The Showgirl Princess

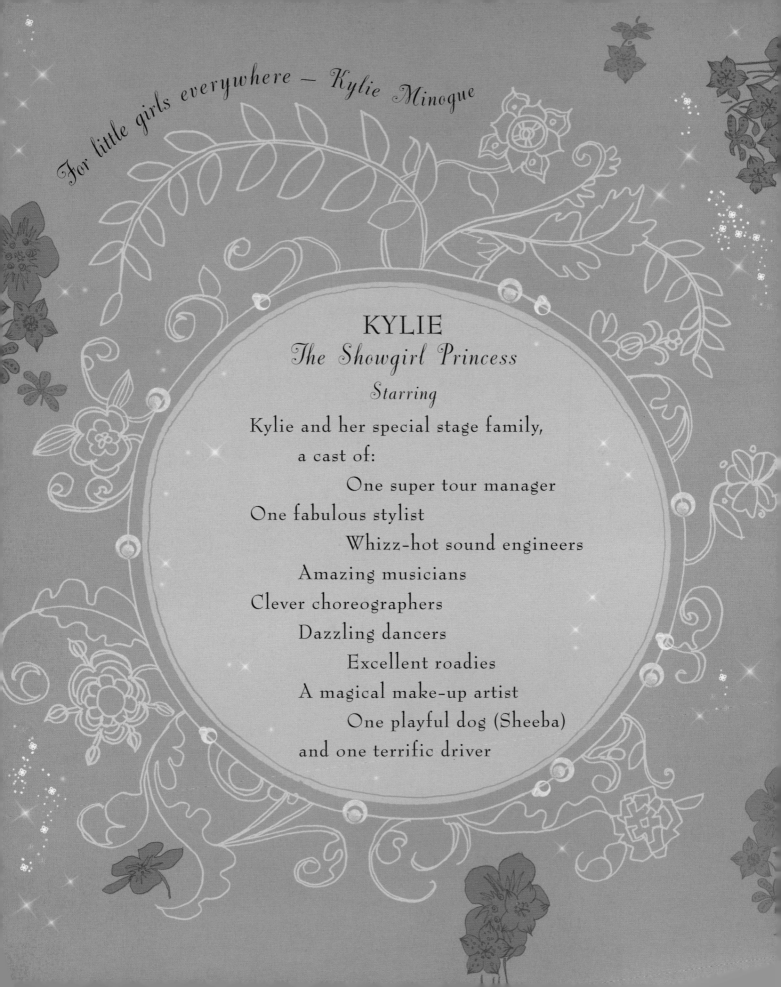

For little girls everywhere — Kylie Minogue

KYLIE
The Showgirl Princess
Starring
Kylie and her special stage family,
a cast of:
One super tour manager
One fabulous stylist
Whizz-hot sound engineers
Amazing musicians
Clever choreographers
Dazzling dancers
Excellent roadies
A magical make-up artist
One playful dog (Sheeba)
and one terrific driver

KYLIE

The Showgirl Princess

illustrated by
Swan Park

PUFFIN

One bright morning, Kylie woke up
with *bubbles of excitement* fizzing inside her just like lemonade.
Today, at last, she would stand on a *glittering* stage
and sing to thousands of people.

Slurp!

Something licked her cheek.

"Sheeba!" Kylie cried, hugging her dog tightly.

"I'll tell you a secret,"

she whispered.

"Today, I'm going to be a *Showgirl Princess!*"

Kylie sank into her jasmine-scented bath
with a big sigh.
Today, all the auditions, costume fittings
and rehearsals would finally come together.
She still couldn't quite **believe** it.

But, thought Kylie, *buried in bubbles*, it was all
thanks to her stage family.
They had helped to make her Showgirl
dreams come true.
"I'm so *lucky* people care about me so much,"
Kylie told Sheeba.

Then an idea popped into her head.
"How about a spot of shopping this morning?" she asked.
"We can get some special surprises
to give *everyone* after the show."

Sheeba **barked** happily.

From now on,
it was sure to be
pure fabulousness all the way!

"*Phew!* I'm all shopped out," said Kylie,
    collapsing into the car.
She had *presents for everyone* on the Showgirl Tour.
        Even Sheeba.

"To the show?" asked the driver.
        "Yes, please!" Kylie said.

But then the worries started.
        Had the stage been built?
            Suppose the spotlights didn't work?
                Was everyone OK?
She reached for her phone . . .

"Everything will be *perfect*, Kylie!"
    reassured the tour manager. "I *promise*."

And Sheeba barked, as if to say,
                "Don't worry, Kylie!"

Soon Kylie was standing on the enormous stage.
Her first job was the all-important sound check.
Kylie took a deep breath and sang into the microphone.

"La la la, la la la la la..."

"Just a little less of this and a little more of that,"
muttered the sound engineer,
twiddling knobs and moving sliders.

"La la la, la la la la la..."

"Spot on," he announced.

Kylie smiled.

Her team was making it all happen.

"Come on, Sheeba!" she called. "Next stop, wardrobe!"

But Sheeba had gone!

Sheeba knew everyone
and everyone loved Sheeba,
so Kylie wasn't worried.

Especially as now . . .
it was time to get dressed!

The costume department was one of
Kylie's *favourite* places.
It was someone else's favourite place too.

Kylie ran her fingers over the rows of *shimmering* fabrics.
Her stylist presented her with an outfit
fit for a princess.

"Ooh la la!" Kylie breathed. *"It's beautiful!"*

The stylist smiled. "And let me get the
sparkly Showgirl shoes . . .

Oh, no!" he cried.

The ever-so-sparkly shiny *Showgirl shoes*
were **missing**!

The stylist was puzzled.
"They **must** be somewhere," he said.
"They were just here.
Shall we ask the dancers if they've seen them?"

And so Kylie and the stylist
ran down to the studio.

The dancers were busy
rehearsing their steps.

"Has anyone seen my
Showgirl shoes?"
Kylie asked.

"Can't you find them?"
the dancers cried.
"Oh, but you can't be a *Showgirl Princess*
without *Showgirl shoes!*"

"You could borrow my shoes,"
said one of the dancers.
"I have a spare pair."

So Kylie slid her foot into a *silver shoe*.
But it was far, far too big.
Her heart sank.
She had to be on stage soon.

"Let's ask the musicians!" the dancers said.
"They might know!"

And so Kylie, the stylist and the dancers all ran to the stage.

The musicians were busy
rehearsing their parts.

"Hello! Has anyone seen my
Showgirl shoes?
They're missing!" Kylie cried.

"We'll help you look for them!"
said the guitarist. He opened up
his guitar case and peered inside.
"Hmm," he said.

"They're not in here."

The keyboard player checked under his pedals. "Nope," he said. "They're not under here."

The drummer looked inside his bass drum. "Dreadfully sorry," he said. "They're not down here either."

Kylie tried to smile bravely.

"I know," said the drummer, "let's ask the roadies!" And so Kylie, the stylist, the dancers and the musicians all ran to the back of the stage.

Soon everyone was looking for
Kylie's *Showgirl* shoes.

The roadies looked in
their toolboxes.

The lighting engineers
searched among
the spotlights.

Kylie's driver
checked in
the boot
of her car.

But no one
could find them.

Where could they be?
Kylie was close to tears.
How could she go on stage
without her special
Showgirl shoes?

"Take a break," the tour
manager said gently to Kylie.
"Let me show you
the moon."

"Watch! If I pull this lever," he said, with a proud grin,
"the moon comes down from the ceiling.
And that's where you'll be sitting!"

Kylie gasped as slowly,

slowly,

slowly

a *shimmering* crescent moon dropped into view.

But there was already someone

sitting there . . .

It was Sheeba!

"What's in your mouth, Sheeba?"
Kylie cried.

The dog leapt down from the moon
and placed a pair of slightly wet,
but still **very** *sparkly* shoes
at Kylie's feet.

"She's just like me,"
Kylie laughed.
"Sheeba loves *shoes*!
But, Sheeba, how could you
give me such a fright?"

"One hour everybody!" the tour manager called.

Sheeba barked as if to say,

"On with the show!"

Kylie picked up the shoes and headed for
her dressing room,
Sheeba trotting behind her.

This was one of Kylie's special moments,
when she truly felt like a *real princess*
in a *real fairy tale.*

She sat at her Showgirl dressing table,
her hairdresser sweeping up her golden locks
into an elegant style.

Next, the make-up artist sprang into action,
with little pots of *glitter* and *gloss.*

And when Kylie looked in the mirror, she was delighted.

*"Thank you so much!
I look as twinkly and sparkly as I feel inside."*

"It's time to sparkle even more,"
said the stylist, his arms
full of shimmery fabric.

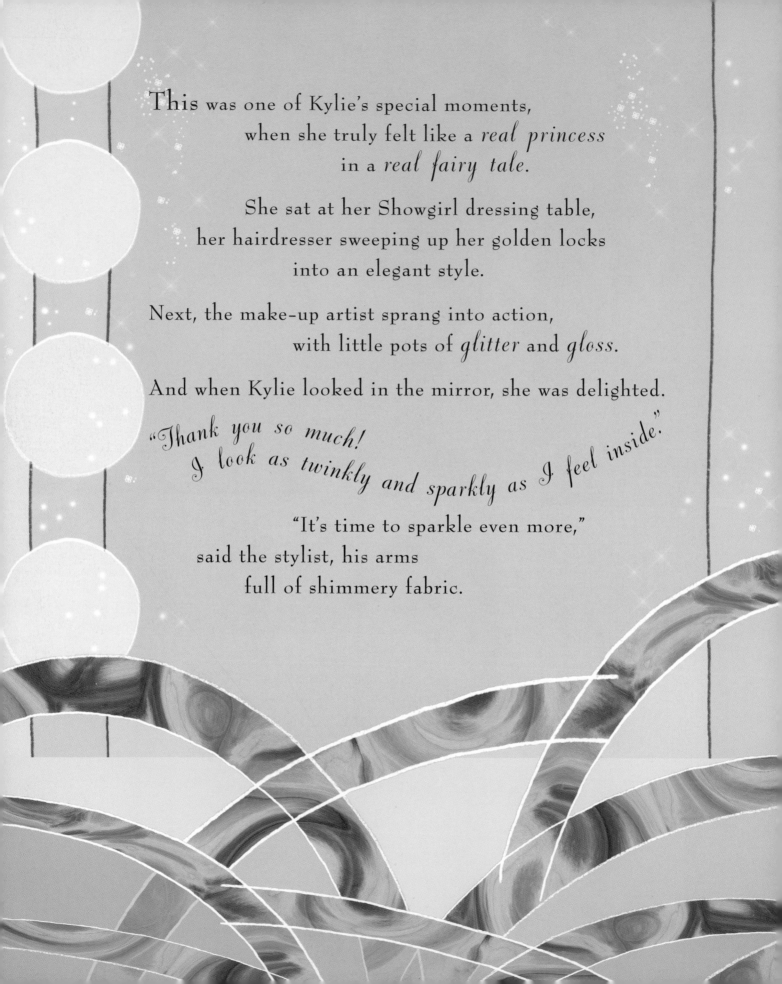

And there was the
Showgirl outfit!

It was truly the most glamorous costume
Kylie had ever seen,
festooned with *feathers*,
and *sparkling* with *jewels*.

Kylie slipped into it, and then placed
the graceful feather headdress
on her head, and, as the final touch,
slid her feet into the
sparkly Showgirl shoes.

"Lucky we found these!"
whispered Kylie in Sheeba's ear.

Sheeba licked Kylie's hand.

The *Showgirl Princess*
took a deep breath
and opened the dressing-room door.

It was time to go on stage.

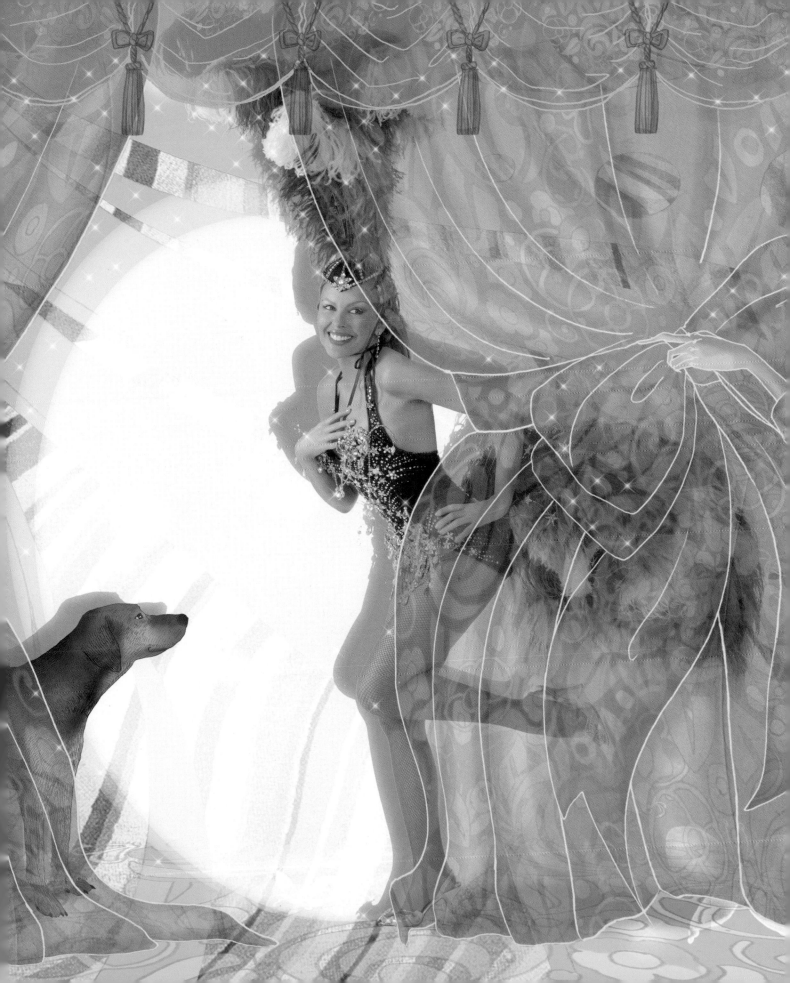

"*Wish me luck*, Sheeba!"
Kylie said,
as her tour manager led her
past the sound crew,
the stagehands and
the engineers.

"Break a leg, Kylie!"
they cheered.

The music grew louder.

Then Kylie,

Showgirl Princess,

stepped on to the stage,
glittering under the spotlights.

The crowd roared.

Kylie smiled and began to sing.

Later, as the magical show came to a close,
Kylie thanked her stage family.

Because of their hard work,
now Kylie really was a *Showgirl Princess*,
just as she had always dreamed.

"La la la, la la la la la ..."

PUFFIN BOOKS
Published by the Penguin Group: London, New York,
Australia, Canada, India, Ireland, New Zealand and South Africa
Penguin Books Ltd, Registered Offices: 80 Strand, London WC2R 0RL, England

penguin.com

Published in Puffin Books 2006
1 3 5 7 9 10 8 6 4 2

Made and printed in Italy
ISBN-13: 978–0–141–38319–4
ISBN-10: 0–141–38319–4